This Book about Undies Belongs to:

To Will, Grace, Kei, Owen, Gardner, Byron, Caleb,
and their undies. — SB

To my Dad, the best undies illustrator I know.
Thanks for teaching me everything I know. — Love, TC

Library of Congress catalog card number: 2016041713

ISBN 978-0-545-87973-6

10 9 8 7 6 5 4 3 2 1   17 18 19 20 21

Printed in Malaysia 108
First edition, July 2017
The text type was set in Rockwell.
The display type was hand lettered by Tad Carpenter.
Book design by Tad Carpenter and Doan Buu

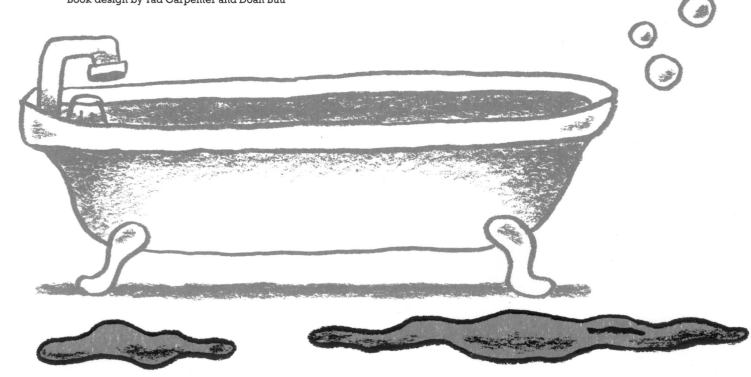

BY SAMANTHA BERGER

MONSTER'S NEW UNDIES

ILLUSTRATED BY TAD CARPENTER

Of all days I dread,
not one can compare
to the day that we shop
for NEW underwear.

I am just FINE
with no undies at all!
Or the undies I HAVE
. . . though they are a bit small.

THESE are my undies!
A sweet work of art!

UH-OH!
My undies!

They just fell apart!

Um . . .

Do you have a small towel?

Or maybe a leaf?

I thought that no undies
would be a relief!

Turns out it feels
just a little bit c-c-cold.
. . . And a little exposed
. . . and A LOT to behold.

OKAAAY! We'll go shopping
for new underwear.
But which ones we GET?
HMPH!
I really don't CARE!

Leave it to MY mom,
'cause only she'd find
a whole store devoted
to JUST the behind!

PUT. DOWN. THOSE. UNDIES.
THOSE. AREN'T. THE. ONES.
Those undies aren't worthy
of dressing these buns!

No shooting stars.

No polka dots.

No tiny whales.

No ice-cream cones.

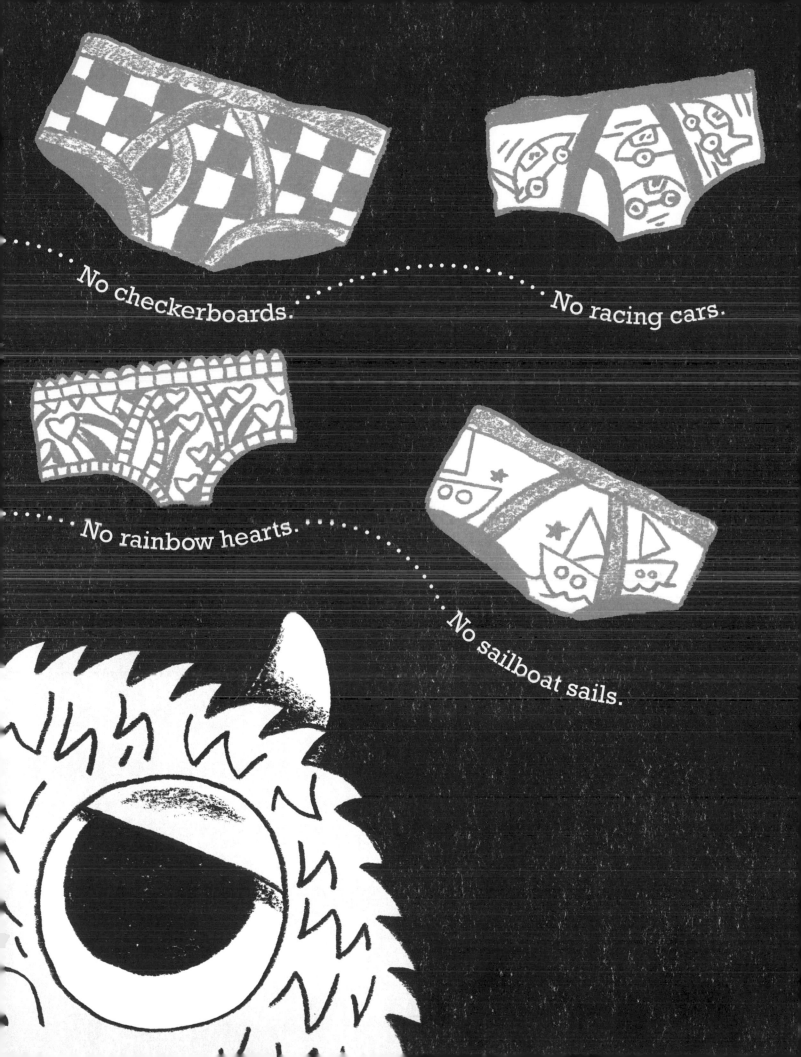

No checkerboards.

No racing cars.

No rainbow hearts.

No sailboat sails.

Those are too long!

Those are too short!

Those look like a diaper!

Those look like a skort!

Those are too boxy!

Those are too tight!

Those are too clingy!

Those GLOW at night!

Come on already!
Can't you just SEE?
There ARE no new undies
just perfect for me.

Please leave me here
in my undie-less slump.
I guess there is nothing
just right for this rump.

Hang on a second . . .
What's THAT on the rack?
Behind all the rest,
hung way in the back?

They look just like mine
but will fit like a glove.
The moment I saw them,
my tush fell in love!

GASP!

Do you know WHAT?

THESE ARE THE ONES!

It's like these new undies
were made for my buns.

I LOVE my new undies
with all of my heart.
I'll wear them until
they, TOO, fall apart!

We'll take seven pairs!
No, make it EIGHTEEN!
They're the most monstrous undies
this bum's ever seen!

And when brand-new undies
are made just for you,
there's something important
you really must do —

The new undies POSE! The new undies DANCE!

The new undies WALK! The new undies STANCE!

And . . . SCENE.